Words by
Jeanne Willis

Illustrations by
Adam Stower

The Wheels on the Bus

SCHOLASTIC INC.

All aboard!

All aboard!

The WHEELS on the bus go **round** and **round**,
Round and **round**, **round** and **round**.
The WHEELS on the bus go **round** and **round**
at the ZOO.

The PENGUIN on the bus goes *flip flap* FLOP,
Flip flap FLOP, *flip flap* FLOP.
The PENGUIN on the bus goes *flip flap* FLOP
at the ZOO.

The WARTHOG on the bus goes
snort snort SNEEZE,
Snort snort SNEEZE,
snort snort SNEEZE.
The WARTHOG on the bus goes
snort snort SNEEZE
at the ZOO.

The HIPPOS on the bus go *squish* squash SQUEEZE,

Squish squash SQUEEZE, *squish* squash SQUEEZE.

The HIPPOS on the bus go *squish* squash SQUEEZE, at the ZOO.

The TIRES on the bus go *hiss* BANG POP!

Hiss BANG POP! Hiss BANG POP!

The **TIRES** on the bus go *hiss*

BANG

POP!

at

the

zoo.

The CREATURES on the bus tip **upside** *down,*
Upside *down,* **upside** *down.*
The CREATURES on the bus tip **upside** *down*
at the ZOO.

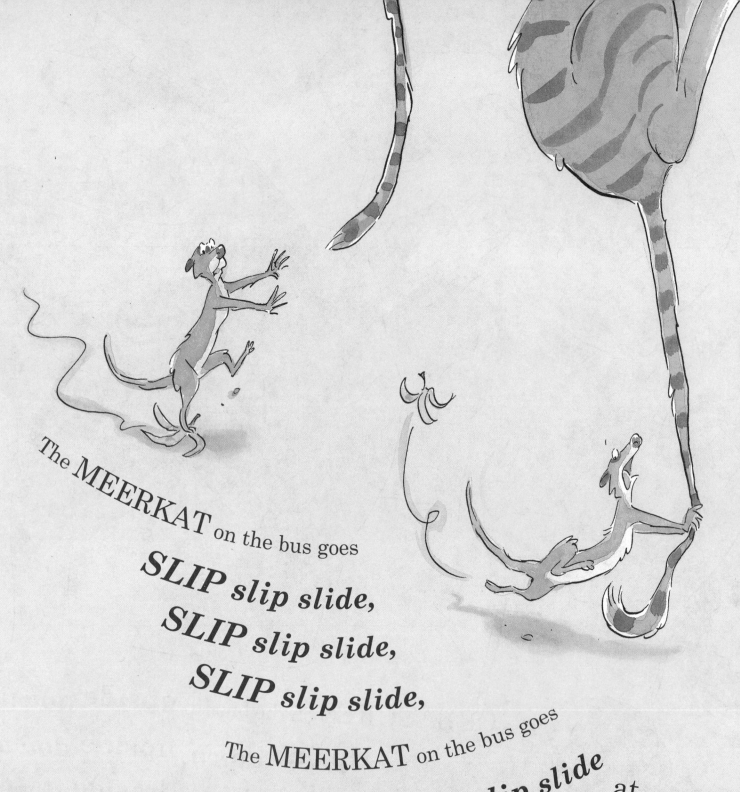

The MEERKAT on the bus goes
SLIP slip slide,
SLIP slip slide,
SLIP slip slide,

The MEERKAT on the bus goes
SLIP slip slide at
the
ZOO.

The TIGER on the bus goes ROAR ROAR ROAR, ROAR ROAR ROAR, ROAR ROAR ROAR.

The TIGER on the bus goes ROAR ROAR ROAR at the ZOO.

The CROC on the bus goes
SNAP SNAP SNAP,
SNAP
SNAP
SNAP,

SNAP
SNAP
SNAP.

The CROC on the bus goes
SNAP SNAP SNAP
at
the ZOO.

The SKUNK on the bus goes

stink stink stink,

Stink stink stink,

stink stink stink.

The SKUNK on the bus goes

Stink stink stink

at

the

ZOO.

The OWL on the bus goes **blink wink blink,**
Blink wink blink, blink wink blink.
The OWL on the bus goes **blink wink blink**
at the ZOO.

"Everybody off.
No pushing please!"

The ELEPHANT on the bus goes *puff puff puff*,
Puff puff puff, puff puff puff.
The ELEPHANT on the bus goes *puff puff puff*
at the ZOO.

The CREATURES on the bus go **clap clap clap,**
Clap clap clap, clap clap clap.
The CREATURES on the bus go

clap clap clap
at the ZOO.

All aboard!
All aboard!
And off we GO!

The WHEELS on the bus go **round** and **round**,
Round and **round**, **round** and **round**.
The WHEELS on the bus go **round** and **round**
at the ZOO.

For Rafe Peacock—J.W.

For Tamlyn, Caroline and Alison
who keep the wheels going round—A.S.

First published in the United Kingdom in 2012 by Puffin Books
Americanized text published in 2012 by Barron's Educational Series, Inc.

ISBN 978-0-545-87729-9

12 11 10 9 8 7 6 5 4 3 2 1   15 16 17 18 19 20/0

Printed in the U.S.A.   40

First Scholastic printing, September 2015